The Eclipse

Acknowledgement: First and foremost, I would like to thank my mother, Johnett, for always encouraging me throughout the course of my life. I would not be where I am today without her. I also want to thank my brother, Malik, for being an amazing support system. My family has been there for me throughout this entire journey and have shared in my excitement. My close friends have given me the courage to go after what I want and I am so grateful to have them in my life. Lastly, I want to thank Troika Publishing for giving me this amazing opportunity to make my dreams come true.
This book would not be possible without the help of these very special people.

Dedication: To my late father, Narvis Ray Ryans who taught me that anything is possible if you believe in yourself and work hard.

The sun and the moon have the most epic and the most tragic story. They loved one another with all of the energy they contained. Sadly, the sun and the moon were billions of miles apart. They could only catch glimpses of one another across the sky when night ended and day began.

They tried to move towards each other
but their places in space were too strong.
They were forced to continue the natural
cycle of bringing the day and the night.

The moon would send the sun messages using comets. In these messages, the moon would say how she wished they could meet and finally be together. The sun sent messages back using shooting stars assuring her that they'd meet soon enough.

One morning when dawn began, the moon saw the sun slowly rise from its slumber. The sun caught a glimpse of his beloved as she fell asleep. Together, with their impossible love, they kept the world and the sky in balance. They had to sacrifice their love to protect the earth and mankind.

The sun and the moon couldn't have been more different. The sun brought day, the moon brought night. The moon was a cold rock and had a dark atmosphere, while the sun was full of hot gas and sent bright rays of light.

Only once a year in the fall, can the sun and the moon ever meet. The moon would travel between the earth and the sun, and see her beloved. The moon prepared for this day. She had counted 364 days for the solar eclipse to arrive once again. She made her trek across the limitless space, and traveled towards the sun.

The moon placed herself between the sun and the earth. The earth had kept them apart for so long. For 10 selfish minutes, the sun and the moon met and casted a dark shadow on the earth. For 10 selfish minutes, they could be together.

On this one day of the year, the sun and the moon could memorize each other's differences. They admired them, knowing that these differences are what makes them special to each other. The moon represents everything the sun does not have and could never know. The sun represents everything the moon cannot be and cannot do. On this one day, the sun showered the cold moon with warmth and light. In return, the moon provided a breeze that cooled and calmed the hot sun.

In a matter of minutes, the sun and moon were dragged back to their original places in space. They tried to fight the pull and begged the universe for more time, but it was too late. They had to leave each other in order to protect the balance.

Once again, the sun and the moon counted the days until they could be together again. They waited until they could fall in love with each other's differences all over again. The sun and the moon's story is the definition of love.

About the author: Bianca Ryans is a fifteen year-old writer and artist who lives in California. Her goal is to inspire people through her words and artwork. Bianca was inspired to write *The Eclipse* when she studied mythology in a high school literature class.
The Eclipse is a classic love story that creatively explains the romance of the sun and the moon.

Visit Bianca at www.biancaryans.com